Daniel
the Devil

To Eamon, Shea
& Dara

Enjoy!
Steve is Com
TASMANIA
Feb 2021

For Edward and Solomon

Bandicoot Books
Margate, Tasmania, Australia

bandicootbooks.com

Cataloguing-in-Publication details
available from the National
Library of Australia

ISBN 978 0 9873840 0 3

Reprinted 2015, 2017

Edited by Jaime Miller
Designed by Shiloh Longbottom
Printed by Tien Wah Press, Malaysia
Text set in Constantia

Daniel
the Devil

Marion and
Steve Isham

All through the night Daniel, David, and Dora played inside the den.

*Round and round and round
chase, tumble, bite.*

The more you
take away the
bigger it gets.

Daniel was the littlest devil in the old wombat hole.

4

At bedtime Daniel squashed in.
"Move over!" said Dora.
"Don't poke!" said David.

Then Daniel slept, safe and snug.

Mum dragged home a fat rabbit for breakfast
and little Daniel crunched the bones.

Made with dinner; never eaten.

When nights warmed up, Daniel, David,
and Dora left the burrow to play outside.

"Beware, take care," said Mum.
"Be sure you can always
see the burrow door!"

ered
taken
ew.

*Round and round
and round
chase, tumble, bite.*

7

"Catch me!" called David, and he dived behind a fallen tree. Daniel tumbled after him.

Daniel couldn't see David and, "Uh-oh!" --
he couldn't see the burrow door either.

"Mum! David! Dora!" Daniel ran shouting.
He ran round and round for a very long time.

"I'm lost! I'm hungry!" he wailed. "I'm soooo tired!"

And he was all alone.

When daylight came, Daniel crept into a hollow log to sleep.
Suddenly a dog's big head blocked the light.

"Grrrr gotchaaaah!" he snarled.
But quick as a wink, Daniel bit the dog's wet nose.

"Woooooh! Woooh!" howled the dog, fainter and fainter into the bush.

Daniel crawled backwards out of the old log, just to be sure.

"Hey! This looks like the log where I lost David."

"And there's the burrow door!" he shouted. "I'm home!"

A beaded curtain hangs in the door.

17

But when Daniel looked inside, the burrow was empty.
He waited and waited, but Mum did not come back.
David and Dora did not come back either.

The strongest thing on earth.

Darkness came and Daniel was even hungrier.

He remembered Mum would say:

Eggs in nest, nest in trees;
tasty treats, when you please.

Daniel scrambled up a tree.

He crunched an egg. "Scrumptious!"
He was about to have another when a large
owl swooped.
Fierce eyes glittered in a scary mask.
Long talons grabbed for him.
Daniel ducked and dropped to the ground.

21

He zigged and zagged, but the owl swooped again . . . and again.
Closer every time.
"I'm owl's breakfast," thought Daniel. "I'm lost!"

Suddenly, a road.
"Whoosh!" A van swept past so close it tweaked Daniel's whiskers.
"What was that?!"

Daniel didn't know, but
it scared the owl away.
"Phew!" he said.

Goes uphill
and downhill
yet never
moves.

23

Daniel's nose twitched.
Sniff, sniff, sniff: meat, fresh meat. "Rabbit!"
After one juicy mouthful, two bright lights came slowly back along the road and stopped.
"Hey little one! All on your own?" said a passing ranger.

Too much see nothing; too little see nothing.

24

"Let's take you home!"
The ranger bundled Daniel into her van.

The more
there is
the less
you see.

25

When she took Daniel out, she said, "Here's breakfast for you."

But best of all: "Dora! David!"

*Round and round and round
chase, tumble, bite.*

"Where's Mum?" asked Daniel.

"She's here too," said Dora. "The ranger's taking care of her."

"Move over!" said Dora.
"Don't poke!" said David.
Then Daniel slept, safe and snug.

*Round and round and round, he seemed
to chase and tumble in his dreams.*

The **Tasmanian Devil** is the world's largest marsupial carnivore. Devils have an exceptional sense of smell, picking up the scent of prey from a kilometre away. Devils run fast. Their short back legs move together while their longer front legs move independently. This gives devils a rocking-horse gait.

Newborn devils are the size of grains of rice. Those not finding their way to one of four teats inside their mother's pouch do not survive. Growth is rapid and before long, pink bodies sprout the beginnings of shiny black coats. Chest and rump will frequently have irregular splashes of white. By three months young devils are the size of newborn kittens; it is a tight fit in the pouch. When they leave the pouch they continue to poke their heads inside to drink. At about nine months old they leave the nest and scavenge for themselves. Devils can eat almost half their weight in food in one sitting. Fat is stored in their tails. Devils scream and make other loud sounds.

Devil Facial Tumour Disease (DFTD) is fatal, showing up in large ugly tumours. It spreads from devil to devil by their natural biting habits. Infected devils die within months of the first lesions appearing. Young devils do not catch DFTD from their mothers.

Researchers are trying to save the devils from extinction through the Save the Devil Program (STDP). Tasmania has disease free devils in Free Range Enclosures (FRE) and wildlife parks.

Did you find these Tasmanian animals?

 Tasmanian Pipistrelle (bat)

 Launceston Land Snail (mollusc)

 Eastern Barred Bandicoot (marsupial)

 Longicorn Beetle (insect)

 Mountain Dragon (lizard)

 Hobart Brown Butterfly (insect)

 Eastern Quoll (marsupial)

 Climbing Galaxia (freshwater fish)

 Tawny Frogmouth (frogmouth)

 Spotted-tailed Quoll (marsupial)

 Tasmanian Pademelon (marsupial)

 Dusky Antechinus (marsupial)

 Forest Raven (Australian raven)

 Echidna (monotreme)

 Tasmanian Wedge-tailed Eagle (eagle)

 Tasmanian Cave Spider (spider)

 Tasmanian Grasshopper (insect)

 White-footed Dunnart (marsupial)

 Masked Owl (owl)

 Long-nosed Potoroo (marsupial)

 Common Wombat (marsupial)

 Superb Fairy-wren (Australian wren)

 Blotched Blue-tongue (lizard)

 Dusky Robin (Australian robin)

 Metallic Skink (lizard)

31

Marion and Steve Isham live in Tasmania. They work as one artist on text and illustrations. Marion draws and Steve paints. *Daniel the Devil* is their 18th book. In their first, published in 1992, they packed the illustrations with hundreds of things to find. This started a habit of inserting extras, especially traditional riddles, that have appeared in their books ever since.

Riddles There are 16 riddles to solve in *Daniel the Devil*.

When first I appear
I seem mysterious;
when I'm explained,
I'm nothing serious.

A quick
creature runs
behind a
picket fence.

Tasmanian Devils open their powerful
jaws 75–80 degrees and snap them
shut to tear meat and crush bones.
They have 42 teeth which grow slowly
throughout their lives.